SKI AT

WRITTEN BY L.A. Fielding

ILLUSTRATED BY Victor Guiza

Library and Archives Canada Cataloguing in Publication

Fielding, L. A. (Lawrence Anthony), 1977-, author
Ski at Spider Ridge / author: L.A. Fielding ; illustrator: Victor Guiza.

(The X-tails)
Issued in print and electronic formats.
ISBN 978-0-9937135-7-6 (bound).

I. Guiza, Victor, illustrator II. Title. III. Series: Fielding, L. A. (Lawrence Anthony), 1977- . X tails.

PS8611.I362S54 2014   jC813'.6   C2014-903995-6   C2014-903996-4

The X-tails Enterprises
Prince George, BC Canada

Design and text layout by Margaret Cogswell
www.spiderbuddydesigns.com

. . . .

Without Nancy Harris, this story would not be
written. Thanks for the inspiration!

And thank you, Vic, for your hard work,
passion, and amazing illustrations!

. . . .

MEET THE X-TAILS!

WISDOM

The smart and responsible lion who is the natural leader of the X-tails. He is a master at solving problems and can fix almost anything. Wisdom loves to "ROOaaaRRRR!" when he is having fun.

CHARM

The cute and bubbly kangaroo. She loves the spotlight and performing at contests in front of big crowds. Her kangaroo legs are perfect for jumping high and pedaling fast. When Charm is really happy, you will see her HOP around or THUMP her foot with a big smile.

CRASH

The clumsy, messy, and very goofy hippo. Crash usually finds himself in all sorts of trouble and is thankful that his X-tail friends are always there when he needs them. You can't help but laugh with Crash at the many silly things he does, especially when he bellows **"GAAAWHOOOOMPHAAAAA!"**

FLIGHT

The strong and fearless rocker gorilla. Flight not only plays the air guitar but also loves to play on any jump he can find. Although he is really big and hairy, this gorilla is a gentle giant. You know Flight is ready for air time when you hear him grunt **"OOOHHHH, OOOHHHH, OOOHHHH!"**

Dazzle

The tough and brave bear who is a tomboy at heart. The boys have difficulty keeping up with Dazzle. And good luck trying to slow her down! She has a big grin, and you will often hear her friendly growl, **"GRRRRR!"**

MISCHIEF

The practical joker of the bunch. You know Mischief is up to something sneaky when you see his mischievous grin. He is a little short for a wolf, so be careful you don't confuse him with a fox—he doesn't like that much. But being small always works to his advantage. You will hear Mischief howl **"aaaaWHOOOOO!"** when he is excited.

And we can't forget about the X-van, which takes the X-tails to the mountains, ocean, BMX tracks, and skateboard parks. This off-road machine can go anywhere and easily fits all of the X-tails' gear. Wisdom the Lion is always the driver of the X-van.

THE X-VAN

"Are we lost?" asked Charm the Kangaroo.

"Nope, we're almost there!" said Wisdom the Lion excitedly.

The curious X-tails peeked outside, squishing their
noses against the windows of the X-van. They didn't
know where Wisdom was taking them to ski.
He had planned a surprise for them!

They grinned from ear to ear. The X-tails loved surprises and they especially loved skiing! Suddenly, their smiles turned upside down when they drove past an old wooden sign.

Dangling by one nail, the sign read: "Welcome to Spider Ridge."

"Oh no!" said Charm. "We're skiing at

It has the **HAIRIEST** ski run in the world—the Tarantula. I've heard that some skiers never make it to the bottom. They disappear into thin air!"

Wisdom laughed. "All skiers make it to the bottom of the Tarantula, but it's usually by sliding down on their rump," he joked. "Spider Ridge is a ski hill hidden deep in the mountains, so hardly anyone knows about it. It has zoober-sweet jumps, tree skiing, and heaps of snow. Besides, we don't have to ski the Tarantula—we can rip it up on the other runs."

Parking the X-van, they all piled out. As they looked around, Mischief the Wolf leaped into the air and pointed toward the mountain.

It was terrifying! It was frightening! It was zoober-awesome! With beady eyes made of rock and creepy crawly legs made of snow, the ski runs looked like a giant spider!

"aaaa WHOOOOO!"

howled Mischief. "My spidey senses are tingling. Let's go rip it up!"

When they turned to grab their skis, they saw a truck nearby. They wondered who it belonged to—a tiger, or maybe a skunk.

Then a zebra rolled out from behind the truck door. She spotted the X-tails and greeted them with her pinky finger and thumb, making the hang loose sign. They smiled and waved back.

They watched the zebra push her wheelchair across the parking lot. As she got close to the lodge, she pulled a wheelie and glided to the front door.

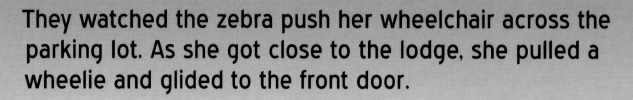

"GaaaWHOOOOMPHaaaaa! That was zoober-cool!" bellowed Crash the Hippo. "What do you think the zebra is doing at Spider Ridge?"

"Maybe she works here," said Wisdom. The X-tails nodded in agreement.

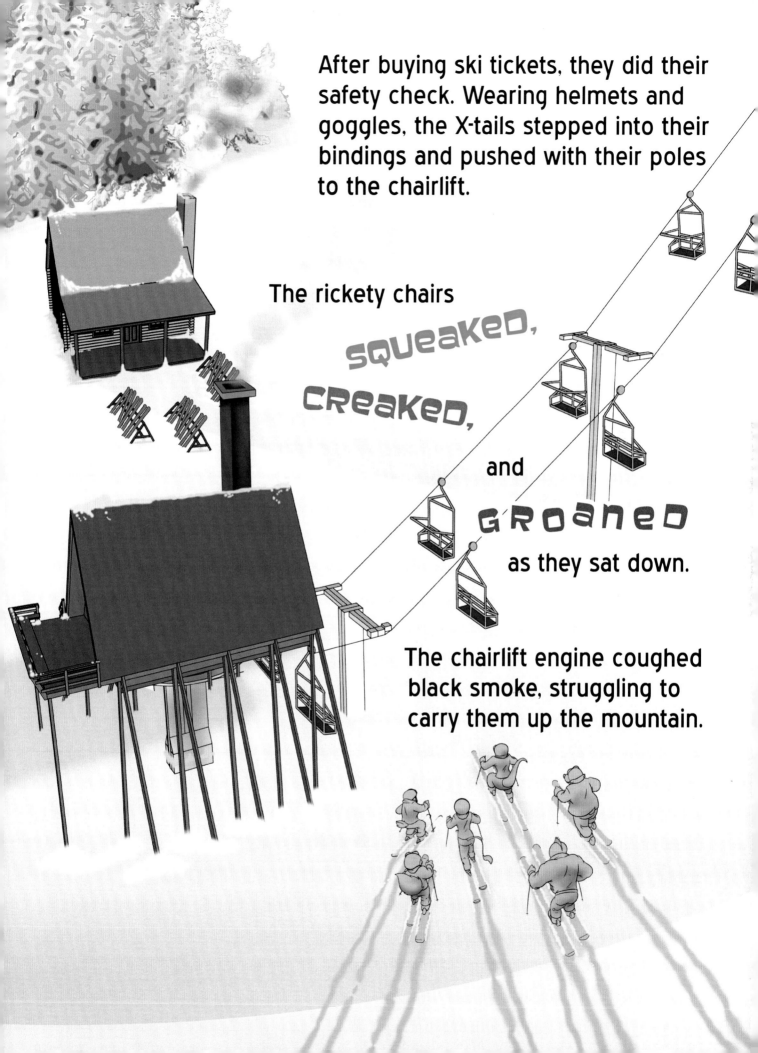

After buying ski tickets, they did their safety check. Wearing helmets and goggles, the X-tails stepped into their bindings and pushed with their poles to the chairlift.

The rickety chairs SQUEAKED, CREAKED, and GROANED as they sat down.

The chairlift engine coughed black smoke, struggling to carry them up the mountain.

Nearing the top, Charm and Dazzle
shivered with goose bumps. Below
them was a steep run with deep snow,
cliffs, and a frozen waterfall.

"Yikes!" yelled Charm. "It's the Tarantula!"

Everyone's eyes widened with surprise when they saw a skier at the top about to drop in. But the skier wasn't standing up—the skier was sitting down in a seat attached to one ski. The X-tails couldn't see who was behind the full face helmet.

"GRRRRR!" growled Dazzle.

THE TARANTULA

"I've never seen ski equipment like that before. It must be impossible to ski the Tarantula sitting down. There's no way!"

To their astonishment, the skier dropped in!

WHOOSHING

through the snow, they heard each turn.
The skier launched off the icy waterfall and the X-tails
closed their eyes—fearful of a huge wipe out.

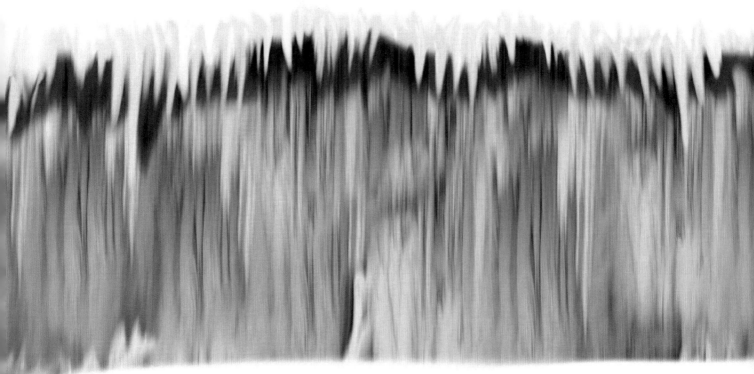

And do you know what happened?

They opened their eyes and there was nothing to see but a cloud of snow. The skier had disappeared! They listened closely and then they heard it . . .

WHOOSH . . . WHOOSH . . . WHOOSH.

It was a perfect landing!

"ROOaaaRRRR!"

boomed Wisdom the Lion.
"Who is that zoober-gnarly skier?"

Arriving at the end of the chairlift, the X-tails didn't dare to ski the Tarantula. They raced down an easier run, with Wisdom leading the way—skiing jumps, bumps, and powdery pillow puffs. The tricks they did were zoober-radical:

FLAT SPIN
SEVEN-TWENTY

LAWN
DART

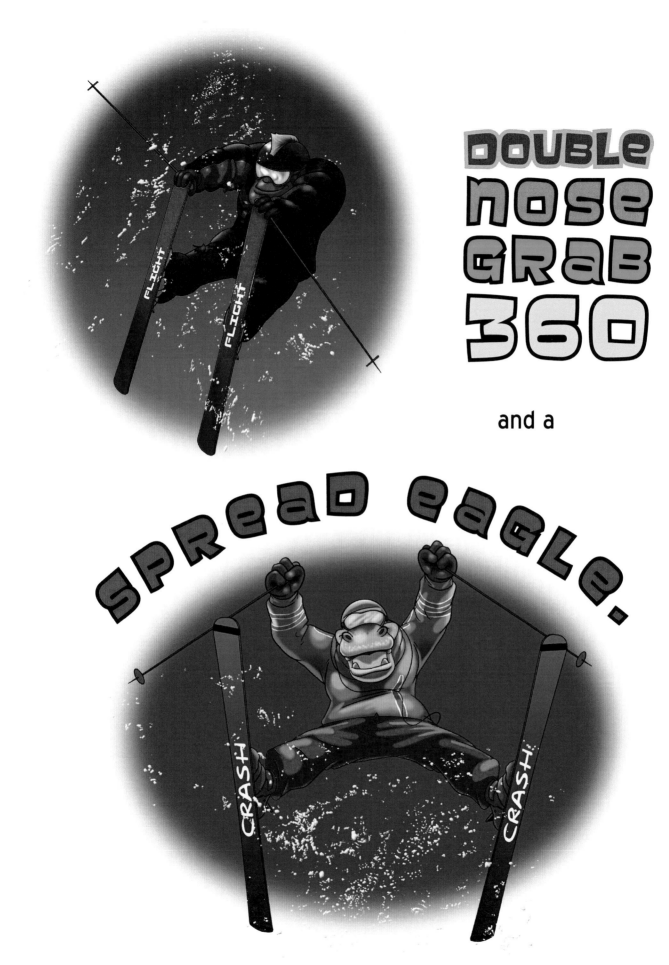

DOUBLE NOSE GRAB 360

and a

SPREAD EAGLE.

The X-tails were zoober-stars!

Zig-zagging through the trees, they saw the mysterious skier waiting at the bottom.

They ROARED to a stop in front of the skier and spoke all at once—"How did you do that? . . . What do you call that thing? . . . Where can I get one? . . . You rule!"

The X-tails stopped talking when they heard a giggle. Taking off the helmet, the skier flashed the hang loose sign at them—it was the zebra they had seen earlier!

Speaking before thinking, Flight the Gorilla said, "But we saw you in a wheelchair. We thought you worked here. We didn't think you were a skier."

There was silence. Then the zebra grinned. "Not being able to walk hasn't stopped me! My sit-ski is just another way of getting down the mountain, like downhill skis or a snowboard. I play basketball in a wheelchair too, and so can you!"

They smiled at their new hero. "You should rip it up with us. We're the X-tails. What's your name?" asked Wisdom.

"My name is Rhumba. Hey, I have an even better idea—how about you rip it up with me? Would you like to try a sit-ski?"

"For sure!" shouted the X-tails. They went to Rhumba's truck and saw sit-skis of all colors. Rhumba explained that outriggers were the small skis they would hold. Picking their favorite color, the X-tails headed for the chairlift.

Rhumba giggled again. "Oh, we're not going up the chairlift. We're going over there." She pointed to a sign that read: "Bunny Hill Beginner Area."

"Really? The bunny hill? Okay, but I think it will be too easy," said Mischief. The rest of the X-tails couldn't help but smirk too. It had been a long time since they had skied on a bunny hill.

They followed Rhumba's lead and couldn't keep up!

Rhumba quickly arrived at the bottom and waited patiently.

The X-tails **HOOTED** and **HOLLERED** as they finally made it down. From their wipe outs, they were covered in snow from head to toe.

"Now are you ready for the chairlift?" asked Rhumba.

The X-tails looked at each other's snowy faces and burst into laughter. With a big toothy grin, Mischief answered, "Hmmm, I think we'd better just hang loose on our regular skis!"

"Okay," said Rhumba. "In that case, let's ski the Tarantula! You can do it, just follow my lead."

Soon they were at the top of the Tarantula.

"HANG LOOSE, DUDES!"

yelled Rhumba as she dropped in.

The X-tails followed her every move, turning when she turned. They were careful not to make any mistakes.

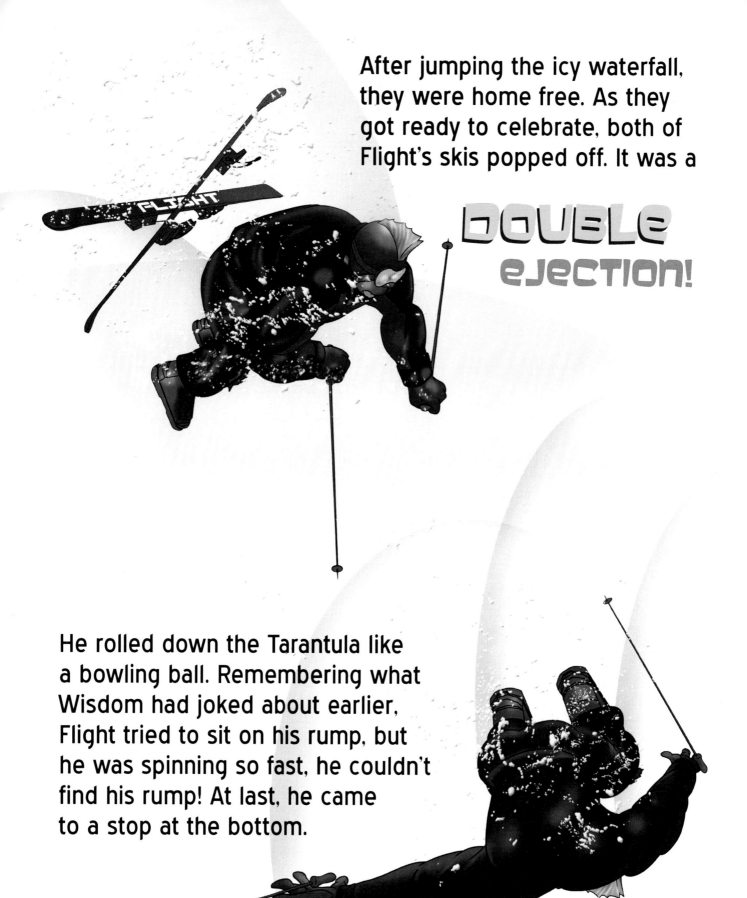

After jumping the icy waterfall, they were home free. As they got ready to celebrate, both of Flight's skis popped off. It was a

DOUBLE EJECTION!

He rolled down the Tarantula like a bowling ball. Remembering what Wisdom had joked about earlier, Flight tried to sit on his rump, but he was spinning so fast, he couldn't find his rump! At last, he came to a stop at the bottom.

Mischief picked up Flight's skis and the X-tails
zipped down to see if their fearless friend was okay.
They got their answer right away.

"OOOHHHH, OOOHHHH, OOOHHHH!"

"Rock and roll!" he grunted.
"Can we do that again?"

"Yep, if you want to," giggled Rhumba, "or you can do something even more hairy!"

"Like what?" asked Flight curiously.

"Tackle the Tarantula on a sit-ski!" laughed Rhumba.

"No way!" said Flight. "Not me!"

"You know," said Wisdom, "we thought you had a disability. But Rhumba, you've shown us that you have DIFFERENT ABILITIES! Let's go again!"

THE end

THE TARANTULA

THE TRICK-TIONARY

BACKSCRATCHER

In the air, the skier bends their knees and moves the tails of the skis close to their back. This old school trick is a favorite of Charm the Kangaroo—maybe it's because of the disco music she hears blasting from Crash's headphones!

CLIFF DROP

It's best to do this trick at ski hills with heaps of snow like Spider Ridge. With some speed, the skier goes off the edge of a cliff on skis or a sit-ski. Make sure to start with a small cliff that has a steep landing. When you become an expert, you can be brave like Rhumba and drop a frozen waterfall!

FLaT SPIN Seven-TWenTY

Flying off the jump, the skier spins on their side for two full rotations. When you're in the air, it's important to lie as flat as possible on your side. Try not to get too comfortable—you don't want to fall asleep!

Lawn DaRT

This trick is a zoober-cool way of doing a Front Flip. Soaring in the air and before going upside down, the skier keeps both arms at their sides and straightens their body like a dart. After several seconds and before hitting the snow headfirst, the skier tucks their body into a ball and finishes the flip. After you learn the Lawn Dart, go for a Superman by sticking your arms out front!

SaFeTY GRaB

When learning new tricks, it's important to start with the basics and the safety grab is one of the easier tricks to learn. In the air and with either the left or right hand, the skier grabs under the binding on the outside edge of the ski. After you learn this grab, use it to stay in control when trying your first Three-sixty!

NOSE BUTTER TRIPLE CORK SIXTEEN-TWENTY

No doubt about it, this trick is new school and nearly impossible! At the edge of the jump, the skier turns and slides the tips of their skis along the snow while the tails are off the ground. Then the skier launches into the air, spinning four and a half times around while going upside down three times—huh? Maybe we should leave this trick for the experts like Wisdom the Lion!

SWITCH FIVE-FORTY GUITAR GRAB

Skiing backwards toward the jump, the skier soars into the air and spins one and a half rotations to land forward. To do this trick with a guitar grab, one hand will grab the tip and the other hand will grab between the binding and tip. Flight loves this trick because he gets the chance to rock out!

THREE-SIXTY DOUBLE NOSE GRAB

This trick involves spinning one full rotation in the air. While spinning, the skier grabs the tip of each ski at the same time. You may want to practice touching your toes first—this trick takes extreme flexibility or long arms like Flight!

ZERO SPIN

This trick isn't a spin at all! Skiing toward the jump backwards, the skier goes straight off and stays backwards all the way to the landing. This trick is easy . . . if you have eyes in the back of your head!

SPREAD EAGLE

This trick was invented a long time ago and it's a blast from the past! On big or small jumps, the skier sails into the air and spreads their arms and legs as wide as possible. Look closely, Crash is making the shape of the X-tails' favorite letter of the alphabet. Can you guess it?

L.A. FIELDING

is an author of children's literature, and a member of the Canadian Authors Association. He dreamed up the X-tails for his two children, while telling stories on their long distance trips to the mountains each winter weekend. It is his family's cozy log home in Prince George, British Columbia, and their Fielding Shred Shack at a local ski resort, where he draws his inspiration.

Growing up skateboarding, biking, and snowboarding, L.A. Fielding now shares the fun of those sports with his family. When not writing or telling stories, he focuses his thoughts on forestry as a Registered Professional Forester. *The X-tails Ski at Spider Ridge* is his third book in the X-tails series.

Other books in the series include:

- *The X-tails BMX at Thunder Track*
- *The X-tails Heli-Ski at Blue Paw Mountain*
- *The X-tails Surf at Shark Bay*
- *The X-tails Mountain Bike at Rattlesnake Mountain*
- *The X-tails Skateboard at Monster Ramp*
- *The X-tails Snowboard at Shred Park*

For every copy sold of The X-tails Ski at Spider Ridge, 50% of the author's royalties are donated for kids with physical disabilities and mobility limitations, which will provide opportunities to use sports wheelchairs and other recreational equipment. Learn more at:

WWW.THEXTAILS.COM

THE X TAILS

CPSIA information can be obtained
at www.ICGtesting.com
Printed in the USA
LVXC02n0309170914
404371LV00001B/2